The Chick
and the Duckling

Translated from the Russian of V. Suteyev

by Mirra Ginsburg
Pictures by Jose Aruego & Ariane Dewey

Aladdin Paperbacks

First Aladdin Paperbacks edition 1988

Text copyright © 1972 by Mirra Ginsburg
Illustrations copyright © 1972 by Jose Aruego

Aladdin Paperbacks
An imprint of Simon & Schuster Children's Publishing Division
1230 Avenue of the Americas
New York, NY 10020

Printed in Hong Kong
20   19

ISBN 0-689-71226-X

to Libby

A Duckling came out
of the shell.

"I am out!" he said.

"Me too," said the Chick.

"I am taking a walk," said the Duckling.

"Me too,"
said the Chick.

"I am digging a hole," said the Duckling.

"Me too," said the Chick.

"I found a worm,"
said the Duckling.

"Me too,"
said the Chick.

"I caught
a butterfly,"
said the
Duckling.

"Me too,"
said the Chick.

"I am going for a swim,"
said the Duckling.

"Me too,"
said the Chick.

"I am swimming,"
said the Duckling.

"Me too!"
cried the Chick.

The Duckling pulled the Chick out.

"I'm going for another swim," said the Duckling.

"Not me,"
said the Chick.